Gary's Banana Drama

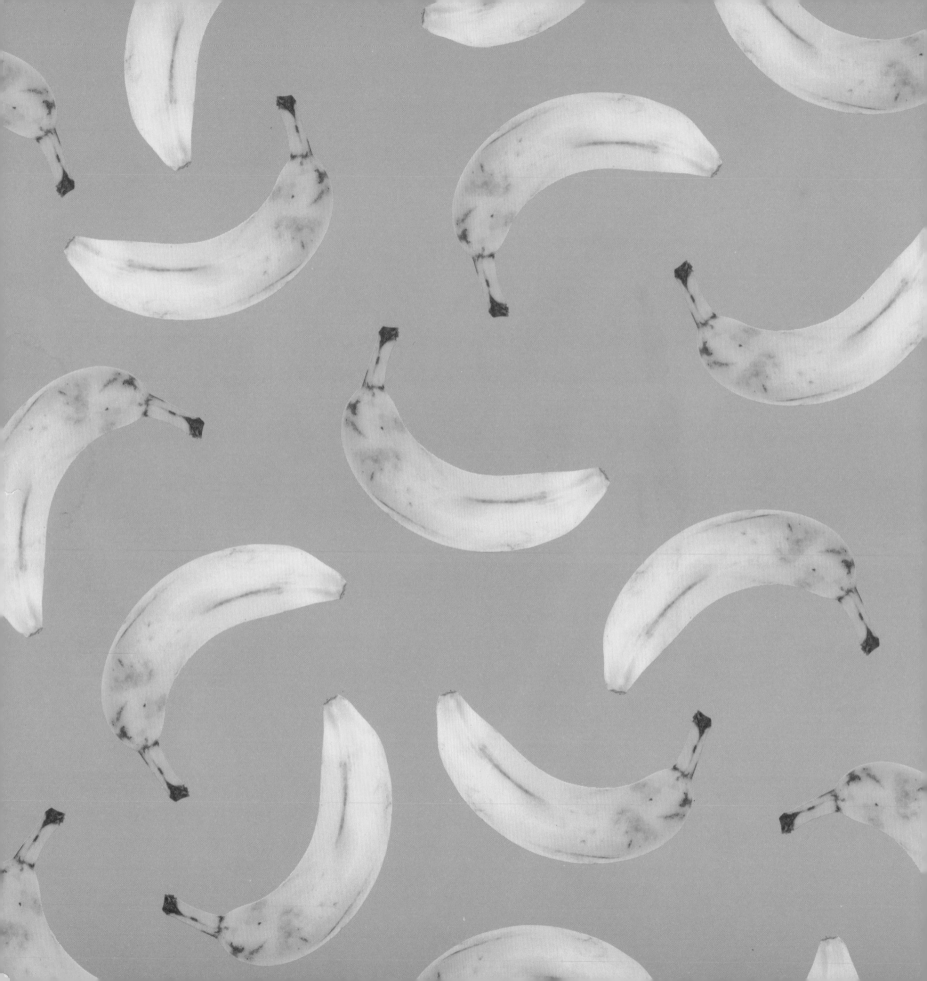

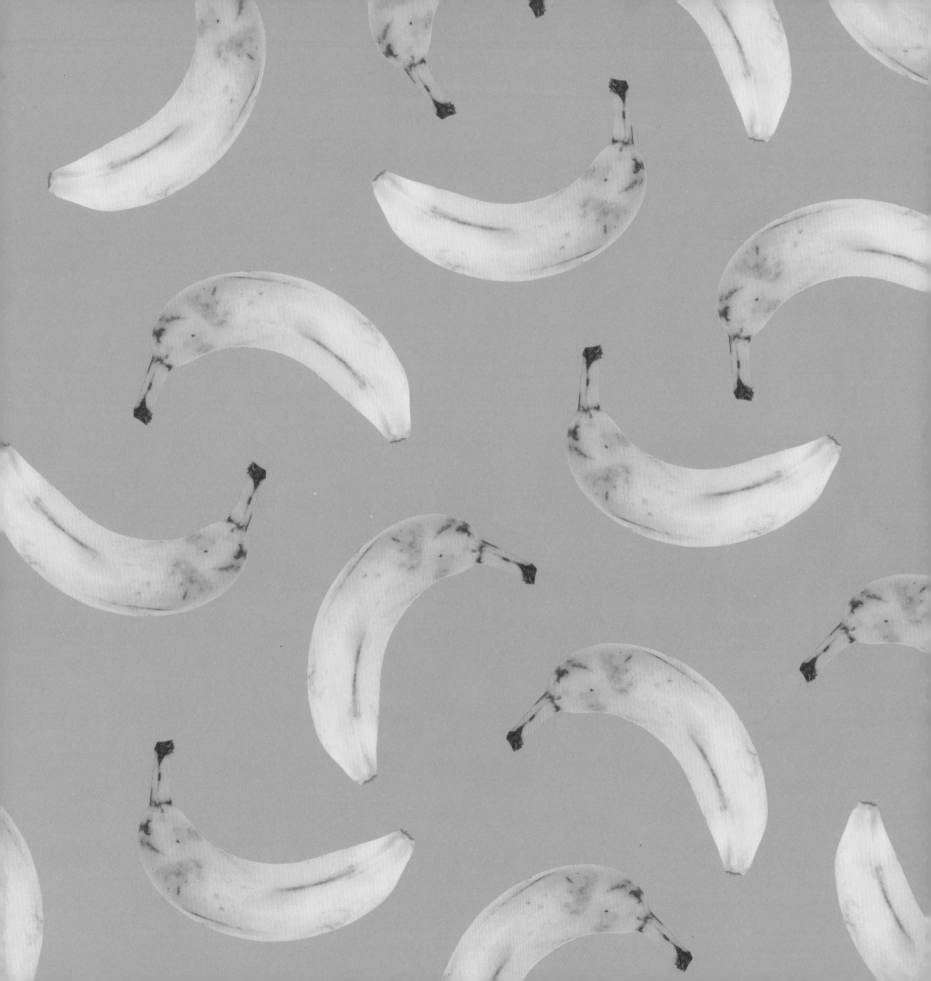

A great big thank you to
Jane Buckley for all your help.

First published in Great Britain in 2018
by Simon & Schuster UK Ltd
1st Floor, 222 Gray's Inn Road, London, WC1X 8HB
A CBS Company

A CIP catalogue record for this book is available
from the British Library upon request

978-1-4711-4784-5 (PB)
978-1-4711-4785-2 (eBook)
Printed in China
10 9 8 7 6 5 4 3 2

SIMON & SCHUSTER
London New York Sydney Toronto New Delhi

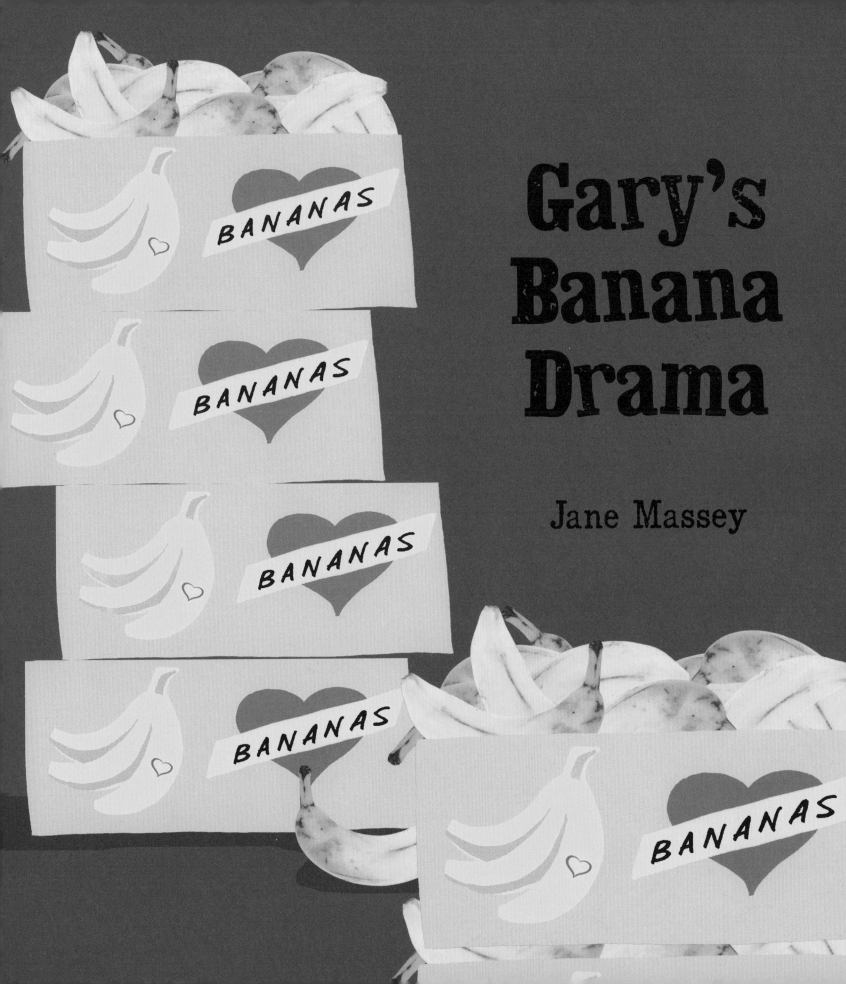

Gary's Banana Drama

Jane Massey

This is Gary.
Gary LOVES bananas.

But one day, something bad happened.

Really bad . . .

There were

NO

MORE

BANANAS.

Any other gorilla might have panicked.

But not Gary. He had a plan.

He put on his brand new hat,
trimmed his toenails, and set off . . .

. . . to look for more bananas.

It was an excellent plan.

Still, Gary was very surprised to stumble across some bananas after only four and a half steps.

"Woof,"
said one banana.

Then it jumped up and licked Gary's face!

That's when he realised they weren't bananas.

They were dogs.

Eugh!

But as Gary wiped away the dog drool, he heard an unusual sound.

Some ripe and fine-looking bananas were singing a beautiful song.

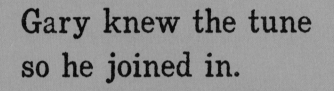

Gary knew the tune so he joined in.

He was just about to take a big bite when . . .

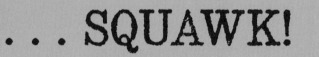

. . . SQUAWK!

They weren't bananas at all.
They were yellow beaks
and there were quite a lot
of them.

One pecked Gary
on the ear.

Ouch!

But there was no time to feel cross,
because lots and lots of bananas were
now rocketing towards him!

BAM,
BOING,
BING!

They weren't
bananas either.

They were **boomerangs.**

"**Yee-ha,**" said Billy.

Perhaps Billy needed
a bit more practice.

Poor Gary was going completely bananas.
He could see bananas everywhere
and he couldn't eat ANY of them.

It was the
worst
day
ever.

And then it started to rain.

Gary was just about to make
his way home when . . .

BUMP!

Had Gary found the best banana of all?

No! It was a GIANT SPACE ROCKET.

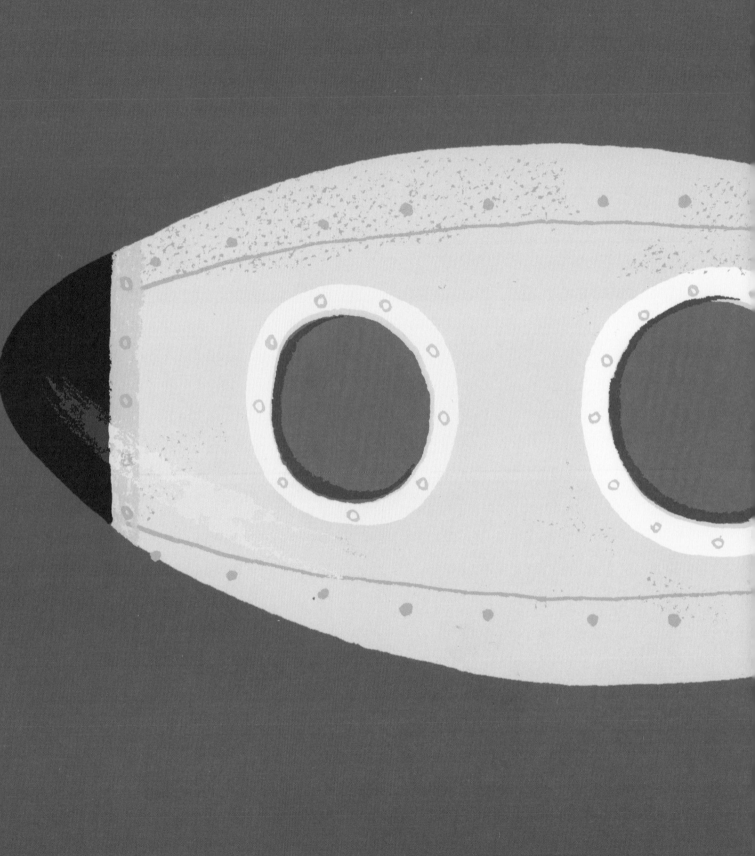

But Gary didn't want a rocket.
He wanted a BANANA!

Then Gary saw it.
High, high in the dusky sky,
surrounded by winking stars
was the most WONDERFUL thing.

Gary leapt into
the rocket.

5, 4, 3, 2, 1 . . .
BLAST OFF!

He zoomed into
the darkness,

and after MANY hungry hours,
Gary landed on . . .

...BANANA PLANET!

"BANANAS! Bananas bananas banaaaaaaaanaaaaaaaas!"

Gary was FINALLY full of bananas.

Maybe it was time to try something new?
After all, Gary had always liked . . .

. . . GRAPES!

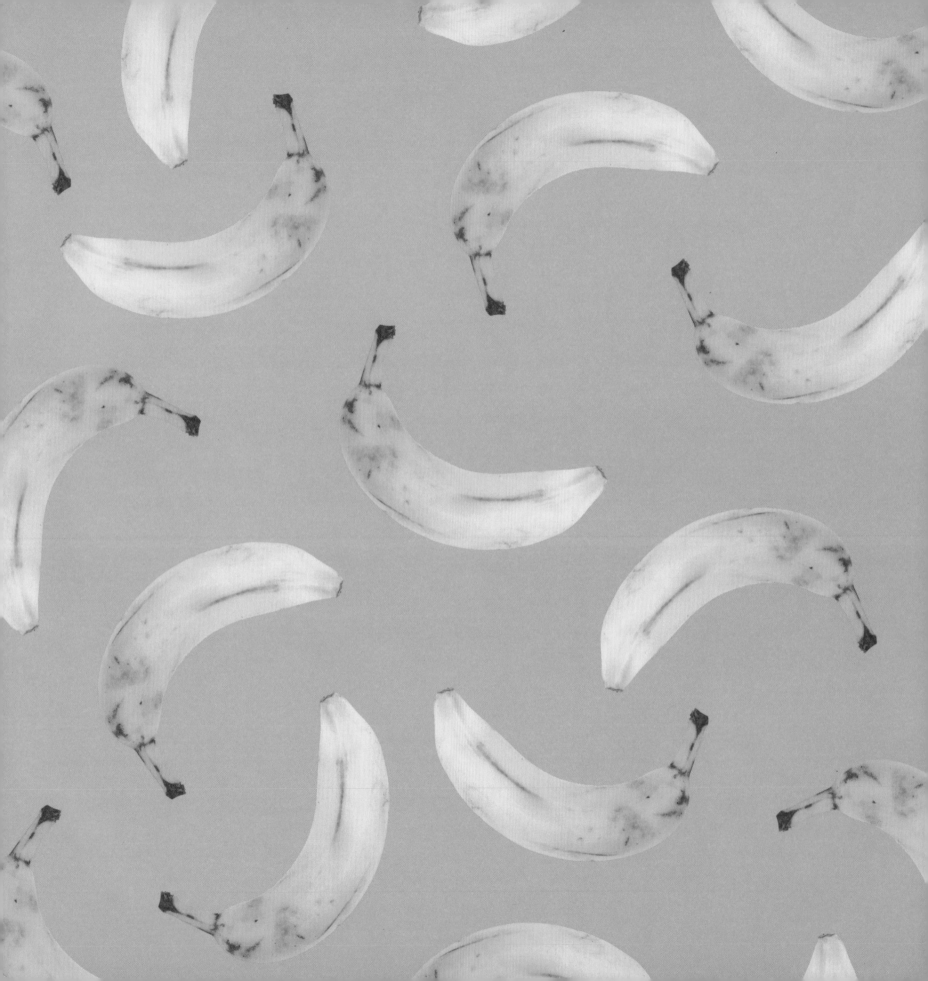